# SERENE BY DAY

## Dhiren R

notionpress.com

INDIA • SINGAPORE • MALAYSIA

ISBN  979-8-88883-983-6

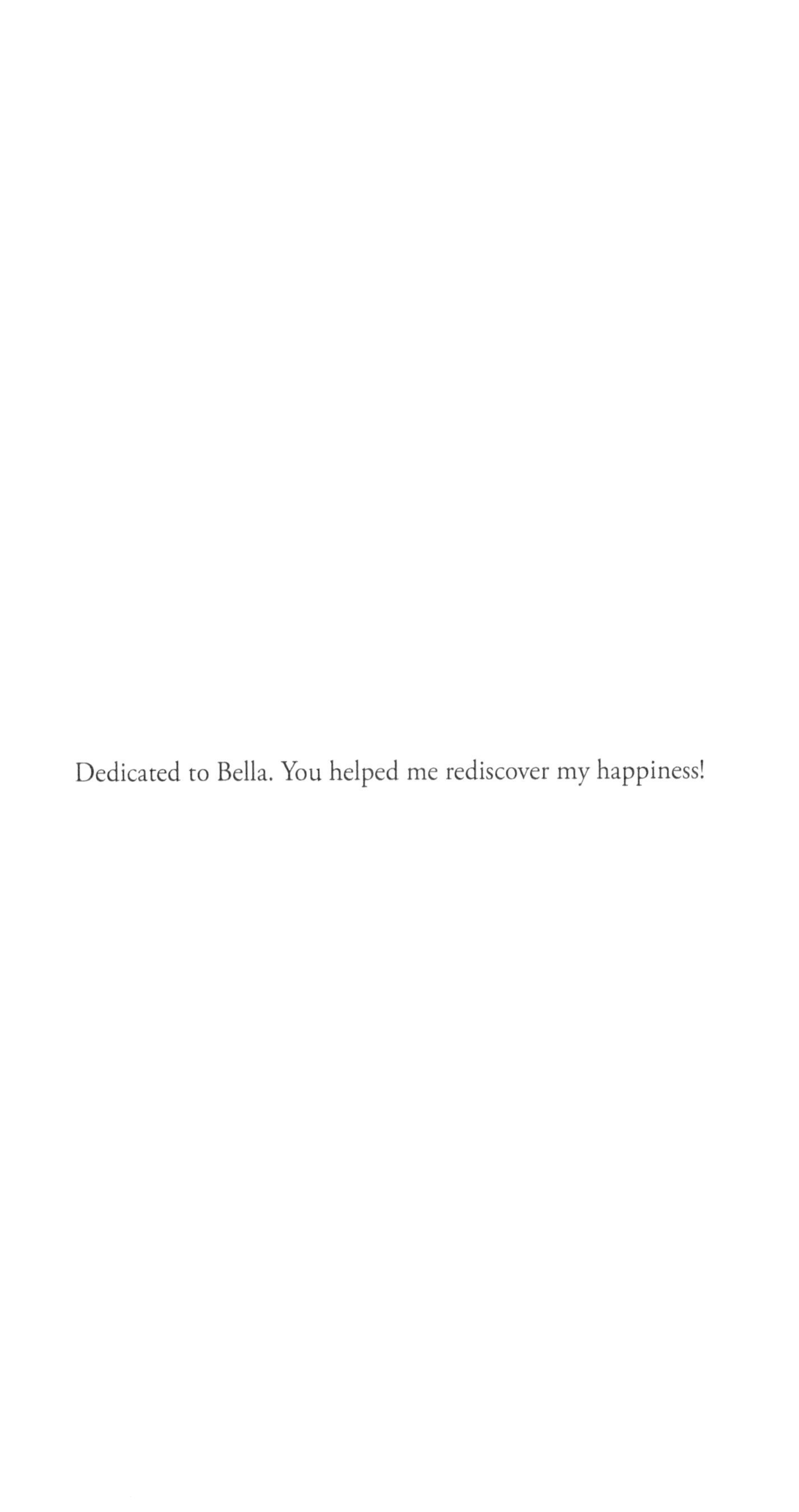

Dedicated to Bella. You helped me rediscover my happiness!

# Chapter 1

"All it takes is an idea, a moment. We all are born equal. We may have different styles of upbringing, we may have come from different backgrounds, but the fact of the matter  is that we are here in this room, as normal people with a common mission – to serve our customers well." The young man, Manoj, continued his motivational talk to a group of 10–15 people staring at a presentation, a few intently listening to the man's words, digesting every word, some penning down his points, while a few seemed disinterested, like they were forced to attend the session.

There was one guy, John, who was in awe of what was happening. It wasn't the talk or the fancy slides. It was just the thought that Manoj had an audience for what seemed like a self-help talk in the corporate world. He gazed at the members of the audience, wondering what brought them here.

The session ended. A few people from the audience had a discussion with Manoj like they'd met a celebrity. A few business cards were exchanged; an attractive woman gave her personal number to Manoj who didn't seem to be really thrilled but still exchanged numbers with the woman.

Realising that the session was officially done, John stepped out and caught up with Manoj who was walking at a brisk pace. As John caught up and started walking at the same pace as Manoj, he asked,

"Dude, how do manage to pull that off? You've been doing this for over two years, and no one till now recognises the fact that you say things that everyone knows, but you still get paid a hefty amount for this stuff."

"What's your point?"

"No point, man. I'm performing tonight. There are chances of a good crowd since the main act has performed on the international scene. Hoping they bring along at least a couple of agents."

"What time is the show?"

"9 pm. Catch the metro to Whitefield and come over to 'Serene by day'. Hopefully, there's no scene this time around."

"Okay. By the way, it's easy to judge a profession by the looks of it. Try doing it. You'll realise it takes time and patience to be a good trainer."

John was a bit dumbfounded. He accepted he was a bit out of line to judge what he saw in the classroom. He took out a piece of paper from his pocket and requested Manoj to review the newly written song he was going to perform that evening. Manoj took it, and thought about reading it but handed it back to John. "Let it be a surprise," he said with a lack of enthusiasm. "Keep it," John said. "You can read it while I'm playing the song."

"That's okay. I have enough pieces of paper in my wallet." John didn't understand

John and Manoj had hit it off quite well. They'd been friends since their brawl at a pub. It wasn't one that involved excessive alcohol or a woman. Both were trying to support their friends who had an altercation over nothing, and in the end, they both realised they were just wasting their energy and decided to get a drink for themselves. A few common interests, the heat of the moment and a few meets did help them become buddies.

# Chapter 2

Manoj was early for the event. The place 'Serene by Day' was crowded; something he didn't prefer. Having distracted himself from people by grabbing a drink, he took a piece of paper out of his wallet, scanned the content with his eyes quickly and kept it back in. After a couple of performances by youngsters on the open-mic stage, he finally saw John appear on stage. John was quite nervous. "Good evening, folks. Hope all's good. I'd be playing a song, one that I wrote. If you guys give a thumbs-up at the end of it, I'd have a chance to play another one. Cover-song lovers, give this a shot. There's no substitute for originals."

John adjusted the keys of his guitar, waited for the recording to start and began his performance.

Ain't gonna help, baby

You tried breaking me

Time and time,

Lying and smiling.

I fell for you,

Lying next to you,

Calling you my pillow.

Not sure why

It scared me while you were away

Waited for the real you.

Dreams, good and bad

Felt they were meant to be.

Tried being normal

That's the most I've tried.

Let's be clean,

Let's be free.

No bricks no mortar

Not about the altar

Just embrace nature,

For she's the beast

Not you, not me.

Try something new,

Wear a new look

Cut the dependencies

Baby, cut them out

I'm the bigger picture.

This thing is gonna start

No stopping you

Not even me.

Will try to run beside you

Can't catch up with you

Coz you are you.

Forgotten the lies

Forgotten the cries

All the stories,

Buried elsewhere

Not in my heart.

As razor-sharp as they come

Divided opinions

Shifting opinions

You know that's me

Need no pills

Just need you

Out of your shell.

"Thank you."

A decent applause followed. Manoj clapped too. John had a smile on his face. Before he asked the crowd if he could follow up with another performance, the host came on to the stage, "Lovely song. Talk about deep lyrics. Let's hear a huge round of applause for John, people."

This time the applause was loud, one John hoped for right after his performance ended. He made his way off stage. Pretty content with his time in front of the crowd, he went over to the bar and asked for a beer. Manoj went up to him and patted him on the back.

"Good performance. Deep stuff, huh?"

"Hey! Glad you made it. Yup, hope the guys liked it. Not like I have an agent."

"Listen, are you up to anything over the weekend?"

"Nothing important. Might expect calls in case my performance was well received. What's up?"

"Have a wedding to attend. Remember the guy who sorted things out between our groups during the fight? It is his wedding. Your presence might work well for all of us and help put things behind."

"Makes sense. Where's it?"

"Wayanad. We'll be back Monday morning. One more thing. You need to book tickets. I'm broke."

"Haha. Cool. You want me to pay for the drinks as well, right?"

"It goes without saying, man. You invited me over here. By the way, I checked for tickets by bus. None available. Our last option is to carpool. Try the app you keep talking about."

The host made an announcement to the crowd that they had to share their contact numbers. In case there was a tie in the results, they would call up the audience members and ask for their votes to decide the final winner.

As one of the waitresses was busy collecting the numbers from the members of the crowd, Manoj gave his and so did the two men who were sitting right next to him.

John looked up the standard websites for tickets. Considering it was a last-minute plan, he couldn't get any confirmed seats like Manoj had mentioned. His only hope was carpooling. He tried a few posts, but all of them had only one vacant seat. He finally managed to get hold of one guy who said he had two vacant seats and the pick-up was convenient too. Quite a short distance from where he lived.

# Chapter 3

Having packed quickly, Manoj waited for John at the gate of his rented home. A bag with clothes, shoes and toiletries is what he was ready with. John took a while in reaching Manoj's place as it was his first time. After he reached, they booked a local cab and reached the spot where John was asked to wait at. They decided to have an early lunch since they had around 30 minutes to spare. They had some conversations about the performance of the previous  night and made plans of visiting a few places in Wayanad after the wedding. They'd known each other for a few months but had never got to know each other on a personal level.

Their ride had arrived. They saw two young men seated in the front of the car, with the guy next to the driver wearing a cast around his arm. The driver noticed John had bags and opened the boot of the car. After getting into the car, they introduced themselves to each other.

"Hi. I'm Suraj, and this is my friend, Rishi," said the guy who had taken charge of the driving. "Hi. Thanks for us picking us up. I'm Manoj and this is…"

Suraj interrupted, "First time to Wayanad?"

"Yes. Going there for a wedding. How about you guys?"

Rishi replied, "We are from Wayanad. We work in Bangalore. Did you guys have lunch?" John, who had a heavy meal, said, "Yes. We did."

Suraj smiled and said, "Great. So did we. We can save some time. Need to make it to the forest reserve check post by 6 pm."

John relieved that he didn't have to wait any longer, said, "Oh, ok. All right, then. We are good to go."

Once the engine started, and the drive had begun, the polite and small talk pertaining to the native town, jobs, work culture, and politics ensued for an hour or so followed by a long silence.

John took his phone out of his pocket and checked to see whether he had any messages on his performance last night. None so far. A bit disappointed, he decided to keep himself busy by penning down some words for a new track. Though his concentration was not at its best, he jotted down a few lines on his phone.

Manoj was just sitting idly, looking outside the window even though the view wasn't picturesque. The guys in front were having conversations on the road to take and whether they'd make it to the check post on time.

The drive was pleasant. The guys made a couple of stops to fill fuel and have tea and smokes.

Three hours had passed, and they finally saw a sign board indicating the check post was a few kilometres away.

Except for two-three instances where John felt the conversations were odd, all seemed content, with no awkward moments. One that kept John thinking for a bit was Rishi's mention of 'Serene by Day' a couple of times and how it is turning out to be a popular place for upcoming artists. All John could think of was that of all places in Bangalore, why would they be talking about a place I performed at last night? Anyway, he let it go.

They were close to the check post. Suraj just requested the guys to throw out anything related to alcohol from the car. Once that was sorted out, they proceeded towards  the check post with ease. They were fifteen minutes ahead of the 6 pm deadline. The customary checks were done, and they were allowed to pass.

# Chapter 4

Rishi: The view has distracted me from the discomfort in my arm. Suraj laughed at Rishi's statement.

Rishi was right. Once the car entered the forest, everyone except for the driver had their eyes on both sides of the picturesque view. Something about the forest and its dense makeup had them distracted.

Suraj: A couple of more hours and we'd be out. There is a good chance we might get to see wildlife. He was right. It wasn't tough to spot a herd of deer just five minutes into their drive in the forest. They were lucky to spot a wild water buffalo that was crossing the road.

Manoj: Let's hope we don't run into elephants on the road. A friend of mine got into some real trouble navigating past them.

There was no reaction to Manoj's comment. The guys were busy scouting for wildlife.

John was quiet. He was transitioning his state of mind from lyrics composition to wildlife gazing. He quickly made a couple of entries into his notes on the phone, kept it in his pocket, and did what the others were doing.

After the initial excitement of 15–20 minutes had passed, the guys started conversing about their previous experiences with wildlife, nature trips and related activities.

The sun was beginning to set. As it became darker, the conversations were reduced. It seemed like they were waiting to reach their respective destinations. They saw a few cars passing by. Suraj had reduced his driving speed since it was a national reserve; moreover, his primary target of reaching the check post on or before time was accomplished.

As young adults, the guys at the back were a bit uncomfortable with their surroundings once it was dark. Neither of them talked about it. They were safe in the car, not anticipating any danger. But it was Manoj's imaginative thought that he shared with John that creeped them both out.

"Imagine if we were stranded out there."

John: Not funny, man. I think you are better off when you are silent.

# Chapter 5

The drive continued for another half an hour. The scenic view was pretty much the same. Not lucky enough to see wildlife again except for the deer, the group got back to having conversations about mundane things.

As the talks continued, Suraj reduced his driving speed, to everyone's surprise. "Look ahead," said Suraj.

The guys in the car noticed another car with a number plate 0110 (the last digits of John's phone number) had stopped in the middle of the road about 100 yards from them. Pretty risky for someone to stop the car when it's dark, thought John. He also observed the number plate with the pocket binoculars the driver had given. His uneasiness was pretty obvious to Manoj. "Another panic attack on its way?" whispered Manoj. John's eyes were still focused on the parked car. He answered, "A couple of coincidences since I got into the car. Something's not right. I need to step out for some air."

"Could you stop the car for a minute?"

"What happened?" asked the guy driving the car. "Nothing. I need some air; feeling a little nauseous," answered John.

"I don't think it's a good idea, man. Another hour and we'd be exiting the forest. Can you hold on till then?"

"Dude," said the guy next to the driver, "a few minutes is all he's asking for," while adjusting his cast around his left arm. "No harm. Moreover, the guys in front stopped their car. Must be some elephants crossing the road."

"It's riskier in that case," said the driver. "What if there's a rogue refusing to budge."

"*Arey yaar.* Just stop the car for a minute, man. The guy's obviously suffocating."

"All right," said the driver and stopped the car.

While he opened the door, the guy driving the car continued observing the parked car with the binoculars that John had returned.

John stepped out and began to take deep breaths. The wild but natural air was a pleasant change. Manoj stepped out of the car to see whether John was fine. "Better?" asked Manoj.

"Yeah. The number plate got to me. It's the same as the last four digits of my number."

"C'mon, dude. Stop being paranoid about things," remarked Manoj. "Do you want to check the other car out and see what the fuss is all about?"

"And get attacked by elephants?" claimed John furiously. Manoj was taken aback by John's outburst.

"Whatever dude. I'm getting back in the car." As Manoj was taking steps towards his side of the car door, he heard loud screams from ahead. It was that of a woman. John and Manoj both quickly got into the car.

The driver turned the ignition on and decided to reverse. The car didn't start. Panic began to set in. Meanwhile, the car in front was heading towards them in reverse.

In absolute darkness, only the headlights from the car served as a source of light.

"Dude," shouted the guy with the broken arm. "Start the bloody car."

"It's not starting, man," yelled the driver in fear. He turned and asked the guys at the back to get out and push the car. John and Manoj looked at each other in shock but decided to step out and push the car. As they stepped out and began pushing the car, the other car reached their spot and a woman at the back asked them if everything was okay.

Manoj said they'll know shortly and continued pushing the car. Luckily it started, and the guys breathed a sigh of relief. With the engine still on, John asked the woman what the yelling was for—was it something they had spotted?

The woman replied with a nod and said, "Yeah. Spotted a cockroach near my foot." John and Manoj stared at the woman in disgust.

John asked, "Why did you guys stop then?" noticing a young man and a woman in the front seat. The young man replied, "My wife was feeling nauseous. She's not fond of driving through jungles. Had to stop for a minute and roll down the windows."

With a mix of anger and relief, John and Manoj wished them a pleasant drive sarcastically and got into their car.

"So much for drama," said the driver. "Let's go." He resumed the drive cautiously this time.

While the exchange of snacks had begun, the broken-arm guy decided to listen to music on his earphones. Manoj had closed his eyes and was in deep sleep since the car-stalling episode ended. While the driver was doing his usual thing, John was zoned out while staring out of the window, trying to make sense of something that was clearly only in his head.

He snapped out of it when the driver interrupted him with a random query on the World Cup group stages.

"I don't follow football. Will probably watch the final with friends after the wedding reception ceremony," replied John.

"That's how the guy over here got injured," said the driver.

John was disinterested in continuing the conversation. Boredom began to set it. He felt restless, though he didn't feel like disturbing anyone. He knew the way he could avoid a conversation with the driver was if he fell asleep even though he was anything but sleepy.

"I think I'll take a nap," he said to the driver.

"No problem," said the driver. "I hope you know how to drive. I might have a take a break in a while."

"Yes. I do know. We could swap places after my nap." "Cool," said the driver. "Let me know when you're up."

John closed his eyes, and this time around, he began pondering over his idea to come up with some new lyrics. He had covered the clichéd love or a broken heart story and experimented with equality and social struggles. He needed something fresh. He knew the music would carve out on its own. While his brain was processing thoughts revolving around new concepts, he could hear some murmuring from the guys in the front seat. It sure didn't sound like English. He ignored it and continued with lines and words he needed to embed in his new track.

The only time he opened his eyes was to check whether Manoj was still dozing, and he was right about it. His attempt to do some serious thinking wasn't really successful, and he decided to put his pretend-sleep plans to a stop and take control of the wheel.

A yawn was enough for the driver to realise that John was awake, and he was glad and had a smile on his face.

"Can you take over now?" asked the driver.

"Sure," said John. "It's time you guys get some nap time. Let me get some helpful forest air and resume."

Manoj wasn't pleased that John had woken him up. His grumpy face was proof of it. But he knew he had slept a bit longer than he should have.

Having understood that he would have to give John company in the front seat for the next few hours, he took a few sips of water from the bottle in the backpack and stepped out of the car along with John. Knowing there would be no more breaks for the next couple of hours, they decided to take a leak and then resume.

A pleasant relief was what John thought while relieving himself.

With their backs towards the car, they heard the engine noise. Assuming the guys in the front were aware that the guys outside were almost done, John turned to head towards the car only to gasp in shock. The car was easily five metres away from them, and the distance was slowly increasing by the second. John shouted, "What the…" Manoj who was now done, considering he had been sipping water every 30 minutes or so, turned to see what the yelling was for.

Manoj gave up the second he saw the car was on its way like this had happened to him before. John tried to run and catch up but to no avail. The only thing he saw while he stopped his short, fast sprint was a hand out of the window and a finger, suggesting an inappropriate gesture. A few seconds later, a white object was flung out of the car, and later the car was no longer seen, thanks to the curve in the road.

John exclaimed, "Great! This is great. Do you have anything to say, Mr. Kumbhakarna?" looking towards Manoj.

Manoj: Why didn't your fast-processing mind think of this situation, Mr. John Nash?

John: I knew something was wrong. I told him that there were too many coincidences for them to be dismissed. Why didn't you believe me then?

Manoj: The last thing I want to do is to break your bones and navigate alone. Let's only hope we don't encounter any wild animals and encounter our kind.

John: Dude… what the hell? You're talking like this is a normal situation, and we can get ourselves out of this with the snap of a finger?

Manoj: Did I say it's something familiar or something I expected? Let's try to stay calm. Let me rephrase that. You try to stay calm so that we can do the right things. You behave all hyper. I can easily use the fact that it was your idea to travel with random strangers against you. Get it?

John knew there was no comeback for that. With his mind clearly not working at this point, all he did was walk a little further with the help of this phone torch and pick up the object which was a caste.

'What a phoney. He faked his arm injury all this time,' said John to himself.

Manoj: Dude, get over here man. Need your torch. Can't see a thing and it's getting quite creepy.

John: What happened to yours?

Manoj: It's in the car. What's the charge left on your phone?

John: 92%. Turning off unwanted things. The network is off anyway. Can easily come up with a bunch of sarcastic ad campaigns that I could pitch to mobile operators.

Manoj: That's the sanest thing you've said or done in a while.

John: What do we do now?

Manoj: Continue to walk, hoping we encounter another car. That's our only hope.

John: Which way? I remember the guy said an hour before we exit the forest.

Manoj: All right.

John and Manoj started their fast-paced walk. With nothing but a phone, a packet of cigarettes, a matchbox, a backpack containing a novel and a bottle of water and the caste, they decided to keep their conversations to a minimum.

The sound of crickets and other insects was something they could bear, but it was the pitch-black darkness that neither of them could fathom. Their silence explained their nervousness. They had walked for about ten minutes when to their pleasant surprise, they sensed a car approaching them. The light of the headlamps gleamed on the straight road, and they turned to see a car coming at a speed greater than what they were used to, even on an empty road. They tried grabbing the attention of the person or people in the car, but the car flew past them so fast that they couldn't spot a single person in the car.

John: So much for luck!

Manoj: Let's continue. Hopefully, the next guy isn't that fast.

# Chapter 6

It had been a dead ten minutes since they saw the car. No conversations. The torch was their lifesaver. Hoping for a light at the end of their tunnel, they stopped for a minute for a quick break. So far so good. No attacks till now. Their only knowledge of animal encounters in the wild was from documentaries and random video clips. This jungle was known for its abundant wildlife and tourism. Their walk resumed and, in a few minutes, they could spot a beam of light around the corner of the road that was curving to its right. The happiness on their faces was back after a long time as John pointed the torch towards Manoj. Manoj too, surprisingly, had a smile on his face. His smile suggested confidence in the approaching vehicle, and that they would be lucky this time around.

They finally spotted the vehicle approaching them. It looked more like a jeep, with its headlamps brighter than usual. They were right. It was an open jeep. While John started swinging his arms as a cry for help, Manoj displayed a thumbs-up sign like a wandering hitchhiker.

It was only until the vehicle was 20–30 yards away from them that Manoj quickly raised his arms up as he had surrendered. He yelled at John to do the same. John, totally confused, quickly did as he was told to. The vehicle came to a halt about 10 yards from them.

"Alle iru," they heard, not knowing what it meant. John heard footsteps approaching, and it was only after the person was in front of the dimmed headlights that they realised he had a rifle pointed at them. The man was dressed in a uniform and stopped a few metres from them.

John was petrified, not moving an inch.

He said, "Sir, English please," as he noticed two other men in the jeep. It was obvious to him that they were forest patrol officers. This realisation dawned on Manoj a few seconds later.

The officer asked in a stern voice, "Who are you? How did you get here?"

John turned to Manoj and Manoj's nod implied that John could reply to the officer. He, meanwhile, flung the backpack to John.

John said, "Sir, we got kicked out of the car while on our way. We've been walking for a while and we're hoping to get a ride if we were lucky. We mean no harm."

The officer still suspicious turned and looked towards his companions in the jeep. He then turned back and said, "Throw that backpack towards me and walk towards the jeep so that the officer in the front seat can check you for weapons."

Knowing that they had no choice, John slowly started walking towards the jeep and threw the backpack.

The officer in the front seat, who has a disinterested look on his face, stepped out of the jeep and began the routine check like a pro. John and Manoj were not uncomfortable with the frisking and let the officer do his job. The officer managed to get hold of the cigarette pack and the matchbox. He took a few cigarettes from the pack that was almost full and was kind enough to return the pack and the matchbox to John. After the job was complete, he lit a ciggie and gestured towards the other officer, indicating that they needed to go back to where they were stopped.

Officer 1: Bag yaar check maadthaare guru?

Officer 2 replied, "College huduguru haage idhaarappa. Ivaratthra en iralla," and checked the bag to find a bottle of water. He placed it back in the backpack and flung it towards John, who caught it.

Officer 1: Show me your IDs. What's that white thing in your hand?

John dropped the caste, got permission to lower his arms and took an ID out of his wallet.

Looked like the IDs eased the situation. Officer 1 had a look at John's ID and laughed softly though the rifle didn't move a bit. He seemed convinced that they meant no harm and slowly lowered the rifle, to the guys' relief. He went back to the jeep and mentioned a few words in his local language over the communication device. After receiving a response from the device, he mentioned something to the driver and turned towards the guys.

"Get in," he said.

John and Manoj, with no hesitation, literally started running towards the jeep like two school boys heading home after their final exams.

Officer 3 (the jeep driver) was quiet since the drive resumed. It had been only five minutes since they sat in the jeep. With officer 1 seated next to the driver, officer 2 had been asking routine questions to John, such as "Do you know the number plate of the car you were in? Do you know the people you were travelling with? The colour, the make etc."

It never occurred to Manoj and John that they were travelling in the opposite direction, they were heading back home. Knowing that asking questions to the officers wouldn't be appropriate, they just answered officer 2's questions.

Officer 1: Since you have seen so much adventure in the last hour or so, you'd be getting into a new one in a while. We could use some bait for our hunt.

John: "Tiger? Sir, could you please drop us off at the next check post? I'm assuming where you guys came from. Hopefully, we get a phone signal, and someone will help us out."

Officer 1: "Over here, especially here, our walkie-talkies are our mobile phones. You don't have much of a choice, do you? We are tracking a few poachers in this area. Be glad we didn't shoot you on sight. Be good boys, for now, don't ask questions, and come along with us. If you support us by being a human shield for us, survive the ordeal in case we run into them, then, we'll ensure you get what you need."

Manoj didn't seem perturbed. John, on the other hand, was about to counter officer 1's statements when Manoj stopped him from doing so.

Officer 1 used his walkie-talkie and uttered a few sentences in the local language. The only thing that sounded familiar was the mention of numbers, those of the car.

It was at that moment that the jeep went off the road and entered the jungle. A road meant for the officers and not one for the public to enter unless they were guided by those familiar with the jungle.

The ride turned into a bumpy one. Officer 1 was right about John and Manoj being left with no options.

John thought to himself, 'was officer 1 serious about using them as shields against the poachers? What if we get caught in the gunfire? Was he just joking? He remembered officer 1 laughing when he saw John's pic on the ID card. Nah, I think he's just fooling around.'

Having got used to the bad road, Manoj was observing the deep interior of the forest. He looked at officer 2 every now and then.

The jeep came to a stop and the officers in front spoke to each other. Officer 1 got out of the jeep with the rifle in his hand and looked at the guys. He pointed towards a huge tree and said, "Here's your temporary home for now. You'll be safe there."

John and Manoj looked at the tree and noticed a ladder leading to a machan on top. They were relieved.

# Chapter 7

As John and Manoj made their way up the ladder into the machan, officer 1 threw a torch and said, "This will keep you up for a while. Pull the ladder up and stay here till we return."

John did as he asked. The jeep continued on the muddy path.

"Time to light one," said Manoj, like they had completed a daunting task and it was time to reap its benefit. While they shared a smoke, took a few sips of water and shared some small talk between them, 15–20 minutes passed. As John got up to explore what seemed like a newly setup machan, both heard gunshots from a distance. Fear started to settle in. Hoping it was the poachers at the receiving end of the fire, they had nothing to do but sit. They sat for another 30 minutes with no words being exchanged between them.

Finally, John broke the silence, "What do we do? How long do we sit out here? I know he asked us not to get down but I'm beginning to get impatient."

Manoj: No way are we getting down.

Fatigue had finally set in. It was more stress than the physical strain that they'd endured. Despite all the fear and anxiousness, both managed to fall asleep, knowing they were safe in their temporary shelter.

Manoj woke up to the sound of an elephant's trumpet. It was morning. The sun had risen. It was a moment he had never ever witnessed in his life. There was something positive in his eyes. It was the sheer sight of nature's creation that made Manoj happy. For a moment, all his troubles had vanished. On any regular day, he would have woken John up to witness what he had, but he was caught up in the moment. He was tempted to use the ladder to go down, but his instinct took over, and he was back to his senses. He managed to wake John up.

It was windy. With no signs of help, it was up to the guys to take a call. They could either stay in their temporary shelter, feeling safe or, decide to head to the ground and start walking.

"Never imagined I would be stuck in the jungle ever in my life," remarked John as he observed a butterfly fluttering past him.Manoj asked, "Do you believe in karma?"

John: Never thought about it seriously. Why do you ask?

Manoj: For nature is the beast. Not you, not me. Remember?

John was surprised that Manoj remembered the lyrics of the song he had performed last night.

John: I wonder what that butterfly does all day. Can it save us?

Manoj: I'm not a great conversationalist. Neither am I a big film buff. But I get your reference. One of us needs to be a wizard to be able to do that.

"Some of these look familiar," commented John, as spotted some ferns at a distance. "What about these jungle safaris? I'm sure they'd run into us or we'd run into them."

Manoj: Maybe. Wouldn't count on it. Got a feeling that the route the officers took was not a regular one.

John: I'm running out of options. As scared as I am to take a stroll in this place, the safari guys are our only way out of this. Can't sit here forever waiting for something to happen. We've been here pretty long and heard gunshots, and considering the officers haven't returned, I'm betting they are the ones who've been shot at.

Manoj: What if we run into the ones who shot at them?

John: The poachers? We aren't carrying anything on us, plus, we aren't dressed like officers. For all we know, they could help us.

Manoj: Why on earth would you even think that they'd help us?

John: I don't know. Figuring out a happy path, that's all.

Manoj: I'm heading down.

Manoj started taking the steps leading to the ground.

"Wait for me," shouted John as he followed Manoj.

The nervousness was evident as they both landed on the ground. They didn't know which way to go. Their mouths were parched, and there was very little water left in the bottle.

There was no doubt they were in an extremely tough spot. Unlike any common problematic situation, this was a one-of-a-kind scenario. But, their body and mind refused to give up. It was more like a misfortune that had turned into an adventure of sorts. Though they were dealing with a real problem, the common day-to-day issues had totally disappeared from their minds.

While Manoj sat on a boulder, John was trying to think of his next move. Suddenly, he snapped out of his wandering mind and said, "We've been thinking about reaching a water source. Not sure if that's a good idea. Don't you think we would run into animals over there?"

Manoj: Go over there or get dehydrated? Need the energy to get out of this problem, boss.

John: Next time, let's make all the decisions when we are up on the machan. I don't like spending a second down here.

John and Manoj resumed their stroll down the  path that seemed like one that was used recently. After their conversation, it was obvious neither wanted to talk. The only thing that seemed to keep them going was the hope of hearing a stream. Thirty minutes without a drop of water, a few cigarettes since the con and banter started affecting their stamina. It was still bright. The sky was visible and there were no signs of rain. Like they hadn't experienced enough. Rains would have made the situation worse. The two were visibly busy exploring the paths to their left and right, like two amateur trekkers whose curiosity was at its peak.

John: Shall we share a cigarette?

Manoj: Don't mind, but we have a few matchsticks left. We may need them to light a fire.

John: Takes me back to my school days when my parents and I went on a camping trip.

Manoj: Only kid?

John: Yeah. How about you?

Manoj: I have a sister. Parents have gone back to their hometown.

A few signs of the stream getting close. Maybe, maybe not. They weren't sure. Lucky for them, their attire made their situation easier, helping them fend off the insects and ever-annoying mosquitoes. While one had a stick, the other used the caste to avoid the nuisance of these insects. Just like two adolescent boys sticking to their natural instincts in nature.

Manoj: Why are you holding on to that stupid caste? As a memoir of betrayal by the dudes who just conned us?

John: You could say that. Plus, it's the only weapon I have, in case I must fend off beasts.

Manoj: Right. Better than a stick. Moreover, if a tiger is about to attack you, it might see the caste and think twice.

John: Who said anything about tigers? I'm talking about humans.

Manoj: ( grinning) An animal lover, eh? Don't blame you after all you've said and what's happened. Must be a pleasant walk in that case.

John: Yup. It's been good. Haven't thought about my next paycheck, the next song I need to write and perform, hoping it would be the break I've needed in the creative line.

Manoj: Ssssh. Do you hear that?

John tried listening intently. There was a smile on his face. The sound of flowing water. They ran towards the sound. They didn't look like two tired men. More like two excited young explorers about to find their treasure. They were finally there. A rich stream of fresh water flows slowly across either side of the land. To their luck, they saw only wild buffalos and a herd of deer. No sight of carnivores or elephants. They drank water directly from the stream and filled the nearly empty bottle. Having enjoyed the beautiful view for a while, they were tempted to stay on longer.

John: Nature at its best. What a view!

Manoj: Couldn't agree with you more. But we need to get back to the machan soon. Can't stay here for long. We at least know this spot. We could always come back if required.

Manoj then made a slow 360-degree turn.

John: I hate to leave this spot. A different situation would have made me camp here or even build a house.

Manoj: Let's go.

They both made their way back. John, thanks to his camping skills, knew his way back to the machan. About halfway to their destination, they heard a familiar sound. It wasn't natural. It sounded like a vehicle. They heard a vehicle. Seemed like it was approaching them. They both climbed up a tree and looked in all directions.

Manoj: There! It's the jeep.

The same jeep that had dropped them off at the machan was approaching fast. John and Manoj both noticed that the driver was frantically trying to control the steering wheel. He wasn't driving well and wasn't in control. As it approached, the driver lost control and rammed right into the tree next to them.

The guys quickly got down and reached the jeep. They noticed the driver wasn't alone. There was a man at the back lying motionless. Manoj went a little closer to the man and realised that his hands were tied and his leg was bleeding. As John went close to the driver, he was shocked. The driver was injured.

"Are you okay? Where are the others?" cried John to the officer.

"Drive," was the only word he could hear before he saw the officer pass out. It was the officer who had frisked them earlier. He was shot in the shoulder.

At the back, Manoj couldn't help but provide some comfort to the injured man, who he assumed was the poacher. He poured some water down the man's mouth and asked if he was okay. The man said nothing. His expression suggested that the water soothed his state of mind for a moment. With his hands tied and having been shot in the leg, he just lay motionless, not speaking a word.

John hopped into the jeep and tried starting the engine. He wasn't lucky. He tried again, and the engine started this time around. Not knowing where to go, he followed the muddy trail.

John had no idea where he was going. Manoj helped by guiding him and ensuring John took the correct road. Luckily for them, some tyre tracks helped them in taking the right route. In a blink of a moment, Manoj noticed a black panther on top of a tree. On any regular day, it might have been scary to go past a wild cat. Today wasn't that day. They had two injured men to save.

"Faster," said Manoj, who was beginning to feel the pressure.

"I can't," screamed John. "We are lucky this jeep is in driving condition after the bump it took. If you are so keen on driving fast, why don't you take the wheel?"

"I'm in no condition to have an argument with you right now. Just drive," said Manoj.

John wasn't in the right frame of mind to assess Manoj's anxiousness. All he could think about was the main road. Both were nervous.

"Why didn't you ever learn to drive well?" asked John. He was frustrated, and the question he asked proved it. Manoj snapped.

"You're not wrong. I've had to turn into a so-called jerk, as some may put it; not just because of the mistakes I had committed. Also because of people who made the most of my pathetic choices and got away with their own rubbish actions and water-cooler talks. The same people whom I cared for and I trusted at one point in time."

John: What are you talking about? You aren't making any sense.

Manoj: No. I am making sense. You've been going on and on about the things I haven't done or should have done well.

John: I believe you're trying to rationalise your actions and put the blame on someone else.

Manoj: No, buddy. I accept my mistakes. Have they done their bit? I guess not. There's no point in waiting for them. Move on! The same advice was imparted to me when I was in denial and filled with rage.

John: Who's the "they" you are talking about and imparted by whom?

Manoj: It really doesn't matter. They call it irony.

He seemed to have calmed down as he grinned.

They resumed their pace. It had been fifteen minutes since they entered the jeep. After a few dangerous turns, keeping his speed in mind, John managed to get onto a muddy but stable road. He drove for a few more minutes quite fast until he saw something he'd been wanting to see. A regular road.

The jeep finally made it close to the main road. After a scary drive with two injured men, John and Manoj looked at each other, knowing one-half of the task was completed. They now had to ensure the injured men reached the check post where they could receive some medical attention. With the jeep having nearly broken down, they couldn't rely on it to take them any further. They tried their luck by pushing the engine to its limit, but it was of no use. The vehicle had finally broken down. Desperate to achieve their task, they used all their strength in lifting the passed-out officer and carried him to the main road. They lay his unconscious body on the side of the main road and returned to the jeep to get the other man, whose hands were tied. The man seemed cooperative and limped along with their support. They breathed a sigh of relief when they reached the main road with the injured men next to them. It was time to wait for the next approaching car.

# Chapter 8

Alok stepped out of the swimming pool, dried himself and headed down the lift to his apartment. He entered his flat, switched on the geyser and checked his phone. He noticed missed calls from two unknown numbers, ignored them and proceeded towards the kitchen to make himself a cup of tea. While in the kitchen, he received a call from his mother. He didn't answer, instead, replied that he'll call later. He then switched off the gas, poured the tea into a cup and went to the hall, switched on the TV and turned on a sports channel. It was 6 pm.

"Time for football," he said with an excited smile on his face. While the match was streaming, he looked at his phone that was being charged and decided to call the unknown number thatappeared as a missed call earlier.

He called the number, and after a few seconds, a voice said, "Hello!"

Alok: Hi. I received a call from this number. Who's this?

Voice: Hello sir, I'm calling from Rx hospital. You have a session scheduled for 11 am tomorrow with Dr.Govind. I called to inform you that the doctor isn't available in the morning. Could you make it in the evening, at 5 pm instead?"

Alok: 5 pm? I don't think that would be possible. Is 7 pm fine?

Voice: 7 pm is okay, sir. Confirming your appointment for 7 pm."

Alok: Yes. Thank you.

Alok cut the call and resumed watching the match. A moment later, he turned to his left and looked at a walker. Next to the walker was a table with some items on it. He looked at the walker and the items on the table with disappointment. Immediately, he switched off the TV. Having seemed lost for a minute, he reached for his phone and called his mother.

Mom: Hello.

Alok: Hi Ma. Sorry, was caught up. What are you up to?

Mom: Nothing much. Got back home a while back. Remembered it was Rohit Uncle's birthday. Wished him. He asked how you were doing. Do wish him. He'd feel good.

Alok: Sure. Will do. Did you mention anything about my scheduled appointments?

Mom: No. I did not. Nothing to worry about.

Alok: Good. Not in the mood to give a history class of my episode.

Mom: Hahaha. Sure he'd understand. After all, he is qualified. By the way, are you taking your medication for the pain?

Alok: Ya, Ma. I am. No need to ask me every time.

Ma: Fine. What's for dinner?

Alok: Ordering some fried rice. How's Dad?

Ma: Good. He's leaving for Rohit Uncle's get-together now. Roshni has gone to her singingclasses. She seems to be still high on her performance last week. Please share the video. I'm sure it was great.

Alok: So was the performance of the guy before her. Ask her to sober up when I'm there. Can't stand her hyper-excited yelling.

Mom: Don't be so mean. It's that age. We've learnt not to irritate her. Took a while though. You should try it.

Alok: Let's see. Remind Dad not to talk about me to anyone at the party.

Mom: The world doesn't revolve around you, my son. Step out instead of ordering food. It will do you some good.

Alok: Not possible. Awesome match at 8 pm. Hari might drop in.

Mom: Nice. Say hi to him.

Alok: Okay, ma. I must go. There's a football match on air. Bye.

Mom: All right. Sleep well. Good night.

Alok: Bye. Good night.

Alok cut the call and looked at his left foot. He sighed and turned his attention to the TV screen and continued watching the match.

An hour later, the doorbell rang. Alok opened the door. It was the food delivery girl. She handed over the food.

Alok said, "Hold on a sec," and quickly headed to the bedroom, reached out for his wallet, picked out a note, headed back to the main door and handed it over to the girl.

The girl thanked him and started leaving.

Alok: Excuse me.

The girl turned around and said, "Yes?"

Alok: How did the security let you in? I never received a call on the intercom.

Girl: I visit this place often for deliveries. The security guard knows me.

Alok: Oh ok. Thanks again. See you around.

The girl smiled and left.

'That was new,' he told himself with a smile on his face.

He walked back to the sofa with a slight limp. Not showing any signs of pain, he opened thefood and started with his dinner.

Alok said, "C'mon guys, you need to win today," as he switched on the TV.

A few minutes later, the bell rang. Alok opened the door. It was the delivery girl.

"Hi. Any problem?" Alok asked in a pleasant tone.

"The note you gave seems to be fake," said the girl and handed over the note back to him.

Alok: Oh. I'm sorry. Really didn't know about it. Give me a minute.

Girl: That's okay.

Alok went to his bedroom, checked his wallet and realised he had only a couple of five hundred-rupee notes.

Realising his bad luck, he headed back to the main door.

Alok: I'm sorry. I don't have the right currency. Plus, I'm in the middle of something.

Girl: That's all right. Enjoy your dinner.

Alok, feeling quite embarrassed about having given a fake note, gave an embarrassing smile and thanked the girl. The girl left, and while she was about to take the steps, he stopped her and asked her for her name.

"I'm Megha," she said and left.

Having missed a few minutes of the match, he hurried back to the sofa and resumed his dinner and the match.

Having thoroughly enjoyed his dinner and the result of the match, Alok decided to call it a night.

Alok switched off the light and hit the bed.

It was the middle of the night. Alok woke up and went to the bathroom. He turned the shower tap on. He stepped under the shower fully clothed. The water was boiling hot since he had forgotten to switch off the heater. He didn't seem to mind, nor did he react to the heat.

He stepped out of the shower, switched off the heater and jumped into bed completely wet and soaking.

It was a dream. Alok snapped out of it. He was sweating profusely. A tad bit terrified, he rushed to the bathroom and switched the heater off. He then turned the shower tap on, and let the water flow waiting for it to cool down, considering the heater was on for a long time. Stepping out, he headed towards the kitchen and had a glass of water.

With the water having cooled down but still warm, he took a shower. Feeling better, he decided to go back to bed.

He wasn't lucky. He struggled to fall asleep.

An hour had passed since he had his dream. Wide awake, he decided to play music on his phone, hoping it would help him fall asleep. He selected a soft song, 'K' by Cigarettes after Sex. With a satisfied smile on his face, he turned the light off and closed his eyes.

The next morning, the bell rang. Alok, groggy from having been woken up by the bell, opened the door. It was Hari.

Hari: What a match last night! Sorry about ditching you. I have a surprise for you. Come downstairs. I have to show you something.

Alok blindly followed Hari until they reached the basement of the apartment building. Hari turned around and pointed behind Alok. Alok turned and saw a brand new cruiser bike parked near his six-seater car.

Alok: Woah. Nice. A treat to these sleepy eyes! Congrats buddy. It's finally here.

Hari: Yeah. Finally. I feel like a college student, like ten years ago.

Alok: So, where's the key?

Hari: Not until I cross the minimum number of kilometres for the first service.

Alok: That's a boring response. Worth taking it on our trip?

Hari: Not so soon. It's going to be your car. Leaving early morning, right?

Alok: Yup. Don't forget to carry your camera.

Hari spent nearly ten to fifteen minutes showcasing his new buy. Alok was attentive for the first few minutes but lost interest later.

Alok: Dude. Can we discuss this later? I haven't had a cup of tea. You know I need it to be fresh.

Hari was annoyed and said, "Fine. Let's go back and see if the highlights are on."

They made their way back to Alok's apartment.

While pouring a hot cup of tea into two cups, Hari observed the walker.

He then turned to Alok and asked, "How are your sessions going on? Any progress?"

Alok: Not sure. Have slowly started building a rapport with this guy. Let's see where this goes.

He took a sip of the hot beverage handed over to him by Hari.

Hari: You know. I had a weird discussion with a new person I met. She didn't visit me to talk about herself. She was mentioning something about her brother planning another act ofmischief.

Alok: Hmmm. What did your gut instinct say?

Hari: I told her it would be best if she brought her brother. She wasn't sure about that.

Alok: Hari, here's what bothers me. You discuss these encounters with new people, something that is confidential. Adhering to your code of patient-doctor confidentiality is important, don't you think?

Hari laughed. "And what makes you think I'm breaking it? Did I mention the person's name? No. Do I have plans of introducing you to her? No. I don't think what I'm doing is unethical. Questionable but not unethical."

Alok: I still think it is unethical.

Hari: If it makes you feel any better, you are the only person I talk about this stuff to. As I know you'd keep it to yourself.

Alok didn't respond as he switched on the TV to watch the highlights of last night's match.

Hari: Let me tell you what would be unethical. I have an audio clip of her brother's conversation with his friend. She recorded the conversation and passed the clip to me. It is quite intense and says a lot about the guy. Her having recorded the conversation without his consent would generally be considered unethical. Keeping in mind that she had the best of intentions, I wouldn't blame her. However, sharing the clip with you would definitely be unethical.

Alok listened intently.

Hari: Anyway, you are more than welcome to meet me and talk in a professional setting. I've been asking you to do so for a long time. Just reminding you.

Alok replied, "I don't see that happening," staring at the television screen.

# Chapter 9

"Let me calculate the numbers. I earn 80,000 a month. I pay a rent amount of 15000. Utility bills - electricity, phone, and broadband come up to 2500. My car EMI is 10000. Home loan EMI is 35000. Expenditure on food and miscellaneous items is 10000. I'm left with 7500 in hand. That is equivalent to 50 packets of cigarettes," said the young man to his counsellor. He was confident in his talk while sitting comfortably on the beanbag.

Dr. Govind had been having sessions with Alok for over two weeks. A seasoned doctor, soft-spoken by nature, he listened to Alok talk about how his week was.

"So, tell me. How's your work been?" asked Dr. Govind.

"Work has been okay. Quite boring. My current project isn't as interesting as the previous one. The previous one was one of my all-time favourite projects I've been associated with in my career."

"And, were you smoking a lot back then?"

"I used to smoke a packet a day during the days of my previous project. Why do you ask?"

"Boredom is also one of the main reasons for smoking. Some people smoke when they have nothing to do."

"I keep myself occupied most of the time. But I can't resist this urge to smoke once an hour. It is more like a compulsion. A habit."

"Have you tried nicotine gum or patches?"

"I have. They haven't helped. I've tried electronic cigarettes too."

"You're young. You have the willpower in you to quit smoking. Moreover, as you age, the effects of smoking will show on you. It can lead to a lot of problems. It is totally up to you to give it up. No medication will help you."

"All right, doc. I shall try my best. I'm actually here this time to talk about my financial situation. As I explained with the numbers, I need to start saving money for my future. It has started to take a toll on my mind."

"Have you considered alternate ways of earning money?"

"It's impossible for me to make time during the week. The only time I have is during the weekends. I need to work part-time."

"That's a good idea. Anything else bothering you?"

"My sleep. I'm turning into an insomniac. I read a lot of articles on the Internet and I'm beginning to get worried."

"Reading articles on the Internet is good to a certain extent. I wouldn't advise getting influenced by articles, especially those that deal with medicine. You should leave it to qualified professionals," said Dr. Govind with a smile.

"Also, I have recurring dreams. Every single night. Some are new, some repetitive. I wake up at odd hours during the night, finding it hard to go back to sleep. Is there a way you can prescribe sleeping pills?"

"Have you considered exercising? Let your body get tired from exercising. I don't want to prescribe new medications yet. If your problem persists for a while, I'll think about it. Exercise is a good alternative to sleeping medication."

"All right, doc. I would need a refill of my current medication. Could you help me out with that?"

"Current medication?" asked the doctor with a puzzled look on his face.

"I was referring to attention," said Alok as he laughed. "I need to find someone who gives me a lot of their time. Someone to talk to. Someone to share my problems with. Companionship."

"Marriage is a possible option. You should talk to your parents about it. Are you in touch with your ex-girlfriend?"

"She's still mad at me. Who wouldn't be, considering what I did? And about marriage, as I said, I'm financially not stable to contemplate marriage."

"All right. Let us focus on one problem at a time. Please put in your best effort to exercise well so that your sleep cycle is set right. Also, cut down on your smoking. Eventually, you will have to quit. I wouldn't recommend changing your job for a higher salary. Not yet."

"Okay," said Alok knowing he had some tough tasks to accomplish.

"Okay, Alok. It is time. Please fix an appointment with my assistant for our next meeting. You can contact me between 10 to 11 am for any emergencies."

"All right, doc. Thank you," said Alok as he shook hands with the doctor, got out of the beanbag and quietly let himself out of the room.

"Alok," shouted Hari.

Alok snapped out of his wandering mind. It was a memory of his session with Dr. Govind a few days ago.

"I missed yesterday's session with the counsellor," he said as he slowed down the speed of his six-seater car as he took a turn around a curve.

"Why didn't you tell me? We could have rescheduled our drive to accommodate the session."

"I didn't feel like meeting him. Plus, I fear my parents will figure it out soon."

"You haven't told your parents yet?" asked Hari, as he rolled down the windows of the car.

Alok was distracted by a herd of deer while driving in the forest area. He didn't respond to Hari's question.

The drive was pleasant. Not a lot of conversations between the two. Hari was experimenting with his camera by clicking pictures of the wild. As he focused his camera lens towards the front of the car, he noticed something unusual. There were people on the road. Two of them were lying on the road while one was standing and waving his arms.

# Chapter 10

"Over there," said Hari as he pointed towards the men. The speed of the car increased as it made its way to the stranded men.

Alok and Hari both got out of the car and rushed towards John and Manoj.

"Is everything all right?" asked Alok as he noticed the man lying on the floor.

"No," replied John. "We need to head towards the nearest check post. These men are injured."

Hari, inspecting the injured men turned towards Alok. "Quick. Let's get them in."

All the guys helped the two injured men into the car.

"So, what happened?" asked Alok.

Manoj looked at John. Neither knew where to start.

"It's a long story. We'll update once we reach our destination."

There was a sense of calm during the drive. Both John and Manoj felt like they were rescued. They didn't say much except for checking on the injured men. Their hunger had worn off. Hari was curious to know what had transpired. He remained calm, though. The drove for fifteen minutes until they reached a check post.

The guys got down and rushed towards a room near the check post. An officer, who was in the room noticed them and got out of his chair.

"What's going on? Why did you stop the car on the side of the road? Don't you want to proceed?" he asked.

John, who appeared calm, held the officer by his hand and walked towards the car. He then pointed towards the injured men.

The officer was in shock and quickly reached out to his walkie-talkie and said something in a language unknown to anyone there. He then switched to English.

"I know him. He's my colleague. What happened? Who is the other man?" pointing to the other injured man.

"We don't know, Sir. We must take him to the hospital at once," said John.

"Dharmappa, Muneshwar," shouted the officer. "Guard the check post till I'm back. Ensure those two guys don't get away."

Two officers, Dharmappa and Muneshwar emerged from the corner of the room. "Okay. Sir," they replied to the officer.

As the guys helped move the injured men from Alok's car to a jeep parked near the room, Manoj noticed two men seated in the corner of the room with their legs folded and heads tilted down. They looked familiar.

"John, come over here," Manoj said softly and pointed towards the men in the room.

John's eyes were filled with rage on seeing the men. He was about to run inside when Manoj stopped him.

"There's no point in doing anything now. I think they got what they deserved."

John calmed down. He took the backpack from Manoj, opened the zip, took the cast out of it and flung it at Rishi and Suraj.

Suraj and Rishi saw John and Manoj. They didn't react. They looked dejected.

A sense of ease passed through John. Seeing them in such a condition made him feel happy. Manoj looked indifferent.

Having moved the injured men into the jeep, the officer started the engine and drove fast.

John, Manoj, Hari and Alok had completed what they had set out to do.

It suddenly struck John that they had to inform them about the officers who went missing in the forest.

"Sir," John said. "There are missing officers in the jungle."

"What do you mean?" asked Muneshwar.

"A couple of officers were in a jeep with the one who got injured. They were the ones who picked us up when John and I were stranded. They took us along with them in search of poachers, left us at a machan and went searching for them. Only one returned, injured and he's the one who is on his way to the hospital. He brought along the other man, who I think is a poacher."

Muneshwar listened intently. There was a comedic presence to Muneshwar, Alok thought. His appearance made him feel that way.

John asked, "Sir, could you tell me what happened to the two men in the room?"

Muneshwar was not interested in answering John. "Can you take me to the spot where they went missing?"

"Sure," said John, though hesitant. He didn't want to go back to the place where they were stranded all night long.

"Manoj, you take the officer along. I don't want to come," said John softly to Manoj.

Manoj wasn't pleased with what John said. "You need to come along. We've been through a lot already and we need to get some closure on what has transpired. You better come along."

"We'll join too," said Hari. "I want to capture these moments with my camera."

Alok nodded. He didn't mind tagging along.

Muneshwar communicated over his walkie-talkie and once he was done with his conversation, he asked everyone to wait for fifteen minutes.

"We'll leave once my backup is here. Someone needs to keep an eye on the check post and on the guys in the room."

"Do you mind telling us what happened to the guys? Why do they look so dejected and lost?" asked John.

"They witnessed nature's wrath. I'm sure they were up to some mischief of sorts," said Muneshwar.

"What do you mean?" asked John.

"We picked them up on the road. They were in tears, thanks t o an attack from a herd of elephants. Their car was smashed. It is lucky they survived the attack."

"Did they tell you anything?" John asked. He was curious.

"They haven't spoken much. My instinct tells me they got what they deserved."

John and Manoj couldn't agree more. They looked at each other and smiled.

"Can you imagine if we weren't stranded and had continued on the trip with them? We might have been in the same situation," said John to Manoj.

"I guess we've been through a similar ordeal," replied Manoj.

Muneshwar's backup had arrived. Once he passed on the orders to the new officers, he gotinto Alok's car.

"Do you know any landmark that we can go to?"

"We know of a machan," replied John.

"I know the place. Let's go," said Muneshwar.

Alok was dull and quiet for a long time.

"Are you okay?" asked Hari.

"I'm a little overwhelmed," said Alok. "It makes me wonder that our problems in urban life are nothing compared to what goes on in the wild."

"You could say that," said Hari as he entered the car.

All the men got into the car. One of the backup officers also joined and sat alongside Muneshwar. It was Muneshwar who decided to drive.

The drive was a silent one. While Hari was busy clicking pictures, Alok sat quietly pondering over something. John was narrating the whole story to Muneshwar. As the car entered the deep parts of the jungle, Muneshwar turned the headlights on. After twenty minutes, the car finally arrived at the machan.

"You guys need to climb and stay on top," said Muneshwar pointing at the machan. The guys agreed. As they headed up the machan, Muneshwar and the other officer drove away into the wild to find the missing officers. The four men sat down as Manoj pulled a bottle out of his pocket.

"Where did you get this?" asked John looking at the bottle of liquor.

"I got it from the injured man when we saw him for the first time. This might help," said Manoj offering it to John.

John passed it to Alok. Alok refused politely. "Not sure if it's a good idea. I'm pretty wound up. I have a lot on my mind right now."

Hari, concerned about Alok's behaviour, took a sip of the drink. "You have been lost in your own world ever since we ran into these guys. Is everything all right? You couldn't expect a better setting than this. We are in the middle of the jungle, experiencing something totally new. I think this is the time you let things off your chest."

Alok smiled. He looked at John and replied, "I've met you for the first time today. I'm not sure whether I'll meet you again once we part ways. As weird as it may sound, I'd just like to thank you both for having introduced me to this world out of the blue. I've been in a sad place for nearly a year, thanks to depression and an injury. But this situation is totally new to me. Refreshing, to be precise."

"You don't have to thank us," said John. "You can thank the two dejected buffoons at the check post, whose actions led to this."

Alok reached out to his wallet, pulled out the fake currency and placed it on his lap.

John was done with his drink. He didn't like the taste of it. Neither did the rest. "What are you trying to tell us here?" he asked.

Alok had a tired smile on his face. "I realised recently that this note is a fake one. Megha, the girl who was nearly at the receiving end was smart enough to identify that it was fake and handed it back to me. Do we all get second chances in our lives?"

Alok didn't make sense to anyone. Hari looked disappointed by the way things were transpiring. He stopped clicking pictures and looked at Alok.

"Here's the thing. Your parents didn't raise you to be a sobbing attention-seeking poser. I get it. At least, I think I do. I apologise in advance in case I'm crossing the line, but I'm left with no other choice. Here's something I would have told you if you'd met me in my office. Unfortunately, you will have to hear this from me in the middle of the forest in the presence of people you've just met."

"Go on," said Alok

John interrupted and empathised with Alok, "You have nothing to be ashamed of. We all carry emotional baggage."

Hari intervened, "I know you're in pain—the fact you've had a relapse in depression, thanks to your injury. You aren't as mobile as you used to be, not independent. It is obvious that you sunk into the 'wandering mind' or more commonly, 'idle mind' phase. You seem to be blaming others' actions for your condition. Isn't this something you realised when you faced similar situations or situations worse than what you're going through right now?"

Alok was visibly upset, "Please don't get into that. It's extremely sensitive."

Hari was in no mood to let things slip away. "Sorry, buddy. I'm left with no other choice. You've been whining and complaining about how people have cheated on you and broken your trust. Yes, it really sucks. Do you think you're the only one whose trust has been broken? What happened to the guy, the guy in you who didn't care about what others said? What happened to the guy who silenced the morons not through words but by action? The only thing that matters is that you achieved those things—call it hard work, luck etc., etc. You did what others couldn't."

Alok didn't agree. "It was all a favour done out of pity and agendas."

Hari: Maybe, maybe not. You are just playing the 'holier than thou' card now. You didn't bitch about real stuff and used to pull people out of their misery by saying meaningful things. They may not have thanked you for it, but they surely respected you, and now you're just killing the respect they have for you through your words and actions, rather, lack of actions.

Alok had tears in his eyes, "I don't know. It's all messed up."

Hari continued, "Same old story. Let me get back to what I was saying. You say you are filled with guilt and regret because you've let your parents down. I know you care about your parents a lot. We know it. But just saying it won't help. Any person, let alone a parent, would be hurt knowing his/her kid has made a huge blunder. Don't even think about nullifying your current situation with your past accomplishments. That's just an excuse. No one is going to help you. Your paranoia and anxiety are real concerns, and I am medically qualified to give you an expert opinion on how to overcome such situations. Please meet the doctor with whom you have a good amount of rapport. There's no point in crying over things that have happened. You've put yourself into a problem. Now, work towards fixing it. I'd like to repeat, don't go around creating problems in other people's lives even if you have no such intention. Your emotions and your words seem to be doing enough damage. You need to try your best to keep your emotions in check and get a hold of yourself. If you want someone to listen to you, give me a call. There could be times when I may not be in a position to answer your call. Please don't assume that I'm ignoring you. Such assumptions could lead to negative thoughts again. Do you get it? Get that pleasant smile on your face, not a fake one. You'll find your smile and will be able to get a good night's sleep when you know for sure when you do a good day's work. You don't need others' approval. You and I both know this.

It should come from within. Now, enough of this extremely serious talk. Let's get back to our bad drink. All right? Cool. By the way, I'd like to let you know that the speech I gave you was the last one as a professional counsellor. I should have told this to you earlier. I've decided to pursue a career in photography."

"What do you mean?" asked Alok.

Hari smiled, "I agree that it sounds random. I've been wanting to pursue something new in life. Money isn't my main concern now. However, there's one last thing I want you to listen to." He took his phone out of his pocket and played an audio clip.

"Is everybody bored at multiple points in their lives? No, this isn't a 'never give up' moment that answers this question. If we set aside social comparisons and societal norms, I'm dead sure that everybody wonders what they're up to. I guess having a job keeps one's life busy. What if the job itself is boring? That's a bad situation. Does the excitement of youth really wear off with time? For a person in his thirties, who has a steady job and a decent income to take care of the bills and three meals, does it take an external factor to turn things around from boredom to bliss? Sometimes, finding a partner is the answer. For some, embracing life on a day-to-day basis helps. Some resort to sports, music and other hobbies. But where is it leading them? Yes, life is all about experiences. But, with multiple commitments, is there really a chance to experiment and experience new things in life? Or is this a midlife crisis? Talking to someone who has experienced this pain provides some comfort. I believe everybody's pain is unique. That's because each person approaches the problem in a different way. Sure, having discussions might help alleviate the burden to some extent. But that doesn't fix the problem. For those who want to try new things in life, gaining happiness from something that was experienced already is not the answer. It is more like the line—try it once for the experience. What's next, then? Laziness is a killer, for sure. But it isn't the only killing factor. But are we all lucky to learn early? Do all of us get the freedom to pursue our goals? I've been told that giving excuses is the biggest culprit. It does make sense. That is tied to laziness. But I'm talking about situations that are so bad that one can't escape them. I might wonder how these situations presented themselves. Were they self-created? Or was it just unfortunate? Either way, a positive way of thinking would only look at mitigating the problem so that there's a relief. I'm looking for answers. To be honest, I'm bored. At the same time, I'm excited about the prospect of doing something new. Something that hasn't been done before. I wouldn't consider myself a bad guy for this thought I have. I'm just experimenting with man's strengths and nature's will. Luckily, I have my buddy who agrees with me. What do you say, Rishi?"

Everybody turned quiet after listening to the audio clip. They were in shock, except for Hari. As Hari kept his phone back in his pocket, John managed to muster up some courage to talk.

"Is it the same Suraj who abandoned us?"

"Seems so. I overheard you talking to yourself at the check post. A small world, isn't it?"

"Why is it that we had to bear the consequences of his irrational thinking and actions? Are Manoj and I that unlucky?"

Hari looked puzzled, "Whom did you say is unlucky?"

"Us," replied John. "I've been in a tough spot for a long time now. Never expected that people are filled with such negative emotions that lead them to take drastic actions."

Hari asked John for his business card. John, who didn't understand the context and the reason behind Hari's question, handed over his business card.

Hari and Alok both read it.

"What do you do for a living, John?" asked Alok, who seemingly was out of his lost world and back in reality.

"I'm a freelancing artist trying to make it big in the music world," replied John.

"Then, why does it say that you are a corporate trainer?"

"Must be Manoj's card."

"Who's Manoj?"

John turned to his left, where Manoj was seated. There was no one.

John was stunned. He could not believe his eyes.

"What's going on? What was in that drink? This is not the time for pranks."

Hari could sense the tension in the air. "We haven't met any Manoj from the time we saw you. Have a look at the picture in the camera."

He handed over the camera to John. John looked at the picture Hari had clicked from the car when he spotted the stranded men on the road. It was John, the unconscious officer and the injured man in the picture.

"I think it's best if you meet with someone qualified who can talk to you and treat you well. Mother Nature has played her part. It's time for you to do the rest."

"How is this possible? I've known him for months," cried John as he reached out for his phone. He felt a piece of paper in his pocket. Surprised to find it, he took it out and read the content.

"Hi, John. It's Manoj. It took me a while to pen this down. Having been disowned by my parents for no fault of mine, I have slipped into a state of confusion. To add fuel to the fire, my music career isn't going great. I've resorted to loneliness and my only exposure to social life is during my interaction with people in the corporate training sessions. I meet people and talk to them, but I don't feel a thing. You need to help me out now. I want you by my side so that I don't feel alone again. I've written a song for you that I'll be performing at Serene by Day. Hope you like it. There will be a day when I know you're not going to be around. When that day comes, I promise to get help, for I'm a man of nature and will. Love, Manoj."

As the guys heard the car returning to the machan, John passed the paper to Hari and Alok. Having read the content, Hari went close to John and hugged him. The reality was sinking into John. He was on a trip with strangers who had conned him. He had spent a lot of alone time in the wild, with nature. His mind knew his friend Manoj was sticking around to pull him outof his loneliness. His time spent away from urban life did him some good. He was now with strangers again, but ones who'd helped him out. He had won the battle, but it was time for him to win the war.

# Final Chapter

Having finished reading the book, Joel looked at Chandru, who was quite nervous, wondering what feedback he'd receive from Joel.

"With over 15 years of experience as a writer, I have to say you've done a fair job as an amateur writer, considering this is your first attempt. I mean you've vomited everything that was on your mind. There's no structure, your English is poor, and the ending is totally cliché. It seems like you want to convey something, but nothing's clear."

Chandru: That's it? I too know that. Whatever you said is right. Damn! I'm relieved.

Joel: These characters in your book—John, Manoj, Govind and what's the other guy's name? Alan… I'm sorry. Alok. Are these based on someone you know?

Chandru: No. These characters are fictional. You could say they are loosely based on some of my experiences. Moreover, I don't remember a lot of it. I'd written it over five years ago.

Joel: Then why are you so late in trying to get it published?

Chandru: There's a reason, but that's personal, Joel Sir.

Joel: I can say with a guarantee that no one will convert this into a screenplay.

Chandru: That's okay, Joel Sir. I'd like to get it copyrighted, as I know there's always someone who'd pounce to steal someone else's ideas.

Joel, who looked angry said, "Don't try to be a smartass! It's all part of the business."

Chandru disappointingly nodded his head and took out a bunch of papers and handed it over to Joel.

Joel: What's this? Another story?

Chandru: This is all I have left. It would be great if you could give this a read. It would take a maximum of 5–10 mins.

Joel sighed and took the papers. "I'm only doing this because you've been pestering me for the last 6 months," he said and started reading the content while taking a sip of tea from his cup.

## Intro Scene

*Medium-heavy rain. A rain-soaked Chandru enters the building lobby and talks to the receptionist. It is around five in the evening.*

*Chandru: Hi. I'm here to see Dr. Neena.*

*Receptionist: Do you have an appointment?*

*Chandru: Yes. For 5 pm. Under the name of Chandru.*

*A person walks out of the office.*

*Receptionist: You may go in, sir.*

*Chandru: Are you new here? Haven't seen you in the last year I've been coming here.*

*The receptionist nods and attends a call.*

*Chandru enters the office and sits on the couch of the psychologist's office.*

*Evening, Chandru. So, what's been happening?*

*Good evening, doc. I have an interesting story. Met someone new and decided to test my free-spirited behaviour with someone other than Renu and*

*Aman. So... It's 11:30 in the morning. It's quite sunny. We are relaxing as we speak. Quite buzzed from the weed. A beer would have been good. Surrounded by greenery. I wouldn't have asked for a better setting.*

*#Flashback. Chandru narrates the story to the doctor.*

*Chandru: But on a serious note, I want to ask you a question.*

*New girl: What is it?*

*Chandru: It's kind of serious. I wouldn't want to ruin your mood now, especially since we're here high.*

*New girl: That's fine. Go ahead.*

*Chandru: I've been thinking for a while now. For a few days.*

*New girl: Thinking about what? (curious if he's going to ask her out.)*

*Chandru: My question is what do you think is God's most beautiful creation?*

*New girl: Woah! That's quite deep.*

*Chandru: I know. This question has been bothering me for a while. So what's your answer?*

*New girl: Nature?*

*Chandru: Ooooo. That's a good one, but no.*

*New girl: Dogs?*

*Chandru: Probably the second best answer.*

*New girl: Water?*

*Chandru: Never thought of that. But no.*

*New girl: Then what is it?*

*Chandru: Nice answers, but I don't think they are the right answers. Do you know what I think the answer is?*

*New girl: What?*

*Chandru: I think it's boobs.*

*(new girl has a grin on her face.)*

*New girl: You know you're lucky I didn't slap you.*

*Chandru: Why would you slap me? I'm just being honest. Don't tell me you're one of those women crusaders who say they hate men and stuff. By the way, that reminds me. I have a friend, more like a common friend who goes around boring me talking about women's rights and how women are suppressed. She's an extreme case. So, I'm planning to piss her off the next time I meet her. I've come up with three statements that might do the trick. Please tell me which one would piss you off the most as a woman.*

*New girl: Is this all an act, Chandru? Or is it the weed talking?*

*Chandru: No idea. Anyway, here is line number one—women are objects!*

*New girl: Fuck you. What's the next one?*

*Chandru: Women belong in the kitchen!*

*New girl: That's an old one. And the last?*

*Chandru: I find it cute when women say they want to pursue a career.*

*New girl: Stop trying to be an asshole.*

*Chandru: It's so obvious, is it?*

*New girl: Do you want to light up another one?*

*Chandru: Nah. This is helpful enough.*

*(She pulls out a cigarette from her pocket and tries to light one. It's too windy.)*

*New girl: Do you smoke cigarettes?*

*Chandru: Nope. Let's head downstairs. Feel like eating something. I'd kill for some sausages.*

*New girl: Yeah. I want meat.*

*Chandru: That's what she said.*

*New girl: Fuck off. Let me finish my cigarette.*

*(Takes 2–3 puffs quickly and stubs it out.)*

*(Chandru is humming No Lead Clover by Metallica.)*

*New girl: Is this your ritual every time you want to become friends with a girl?*

*(Chuckles.)*

*Chandru: I don't like smoking up with random people. You're an exception.*

*New girl: How come?*

*Chandru: Will tell you later.*

*New girl: Who else do you smoke up with?*

*Chandru: I hate doing it alone. I'm comfortable smoking up with my girlfriend and my childhood friend.*

*New girl: You didn't tell me you have a girlfriend.*

*Chandru: Why would that be news?*

*New girl: Not really. Was just curious.*

*Chandru: So how's it been in this town? Been two weeks, right?*

*New girl: Was kind of nervous. But it's getting better.*

*Chandru: Good to know. How do you know Arya? She had never mentioned about you to me.*

*New girl: Hehe. Probably because we weren't in touch for a few years. It was nice reconnecting with her.*

*Chandru: Yeah. She's great. Bit of a drama queen but that adds to the entertainment.*

*New girl: Haha. True. She has told me a lot about you. One of the nicest guys she has known is what she told me. Quite an achiever is something she's told me. That's why I don't buy any of the stuff you told me about before.*

*Chandru: Achiever? Not sure about that.*

*New girl: I've also been told about how you've managed to piss her off a bunch of times for getting her into trouble with her friends.*

*Chandru: It's not my fault that she has pretty friends.*

*New girl: You actually fooled around with three of her friends.*

*Chandru: Man! There are always two sides to a story.*

*New girl: And this was before you met your girlfriend?*

*Chandru: You think I'd cheat on my sweetheart?*

*New girl: I didn't mean that. What's her name?*

*Chandru: Renu.*

*New girl: Where is she?*

*Chandru: In Mumbai.*

*New girl: Oh! Long distance relationship, eh?*

*Chandru: That's the sad part.*

*(Flashback ends. Back to the doc scene.)*

*Doc: So, how did you feel? Any paranoia?*

*Chandru: None.*

*Doc: I'm still going to remind you that marijuana is not the right choice. At least not now.*

*Chandru: That's what my previous doc said. But my gut tells me everything's fine. Nothing to worry about, doc.*

*Doc: It's your life, Chandru. I can't force you. So, how's Renu? Did you guys make up?*

*Chandru: Yes, we did. I apologised. But she doesn't know about this new friend I made.*

*Doc: Are you attracted to this new friend?*

*Chandru: She is an attractive girl, but I personally am not attracted. That's the truth.*

*Doc: Nice to know you don't smoke cigarettes anymore.*

*Chandru: I know. Feels good.*

*Doc: But why did you lie to her about your girlfriend being in Mumbai and you guys having a long-distance relationship?*

*Chandru: I didn't get a good vibe from her. She was asking me a lot of questions and saying good things about me that she had heard from our common friend with whom she reconnected after years. I wasn't comfortable. I decided to give some false information just to figure out if she was a blabbermouth.*

*Doc: Given a chance, would you smoke up with her again?*

*Chandru: I don't think so. I just played my routine.*

*Doc: This is something that you do when you're high, isn't it?*

*Chandru: Don't know. Maybe.*

*The conversation goes on for about 10–15 mins and Chandru steps out with a smile on his face. He says 'good night' to the receptionist, and while walking out he remembers that he has left his umbrella in the doctor's office. He immediately rushes back. The receptionist tries to stop him but isn't lucky. Chandru barges in and sees the doctor dozing. He smells marijuana.*

*Doc: Uh oh. Busted!*

*Chandru: Doc! You told me you were on a break. What the hell, man?*

*Doc: I snapped, okay? Here. Want a couple of drags?*

*Chandru.: I don't get it. You tell me to refrain from it, and now you're offering it to me?*

*Doc: I'm tired, Chandru. Tired of trying to help people. But you're my favourite. It's not the pot that made you have a nervous breakdown. You know that very well.*

*Chandru: Then why did you ask me to refrain from doing it?*

*Doc: Coz it would make the diagnosis hard.*

*Chandru: Now that I'm connecting the dots, would it be a fair assumption to say you hired a new receptionist coz your old one found out about your weed activities?*

*Doc: Yup. Anyway, heading home now.*

*Looks out of the window and sees it is still raining.*

*Doc: Do you want me to drop you home?*

*Chandru: That's okay. You could do me a favour, though. Give me a clean chit. I feel like I'm under some court-ordered therapy sessions.*

*Doc: Let me think about giving you a clean chit. But first, let me drop you home.*

*As the rain gets heavier, they get into the car. While driving slowly, the doc says, "What are you doing tomorrow night?"*

*Chandru: Nothing much. Why?*

*Doc: Want to attend a talk show?*

*Chandru: Who's hosting?*

*Doc: Jacob Newman*

*Chandru: Woah! Sure, I'm in. Who's the guest, and how did you manage to get entry?*

*Doc: The producer's son meets me for therapy. Plus, my wife's not interested in talk shows.*

*Chandru: Who's the guest?*

*Doc: Don't know. Don't care.*

*Chandru: Why do you want to go anyway?*

*Doc: Jacob's son has been pestering me for weeks. Says it's fun.*

*Chandru: Should be fun.*

*Chandru reaches his home and says good night to the doc… to be continued.*

Joel had a smile on his face after having read the story.

Joel: Abrupt ending. I'm guessing you don't know how to go on with this.

Chandru: You're right. But I do have a lot of crazy ideas in my mind.

Joel: Well! Then continue writing. I found this small write-up way better than your previous crap. What's with the random notes and keywords in the last bit?

Chandru: Just some pointers for myself so that I don't get too sucked into certain sensitive and dangerous topics.

Joel: Dangerous? Do you mean things like spirituality and purpose, based on what you've scribbled?

Chandru: Yup.

Joel: What's this? 50/20!

Chandru: That's probably the reason I burnt a lot of bridges. That sounds like what a poser would say, but I feel it's true.

Joel: Hmmm. I'll give you the benefit of the doubt. Would you care to explain?

Chandru: Not now. Let me explain the story by writing about it.

Joel: You're pushing your luck now. I'll give you a week. What's this? 'The Curtain Call.'

Chandru laughed and replied, "That's the outcome of me connecting unrelated events in my life. Persecutory in nature, but would get a 9 out of 10 in terms of imagination as repeatedly told by a person I met recently."

Joel: Now this is getting a bit annoying, man!

Chandru: It's okay, Joel Sir. The fact that a person like you spared 30 minutes for me is something I'm happy about.

Chandru finished his cup of tea, placed it next to the cup that Joel had drank from and got up from his chair. Having wished Joel a good day, he left the room and breathed a sigh of relief. He could hear Joel uncontrollably coughing loudly, and after a few seconds, it stopped abruptly. He knew the outcome of his meeting with Joel was a successful one. That is all he had wished for. His smile was back, this time for good. He re-entered the room, and his smile was wider when he saw Joel passed out on the floor with blood stains all over his mouth and on the floor.

www.ingramcontent.com/pod-product-compliance
Lightning Source LLC
Chambersburg PA
CBHW031334130726
47988CB00007B/3125